To Sophia and Theo, with love – *B.H.*
To Amber and David, with love – *E.D.*

First published in Great Britain and in the USA in 2010 by
Frances Lincoln Children's Books, 4 Torriano Mews,
Torriano Avenue, London NW5 2RZ
www.franceslincoln.com

British Library Cataloguing in Publication Data available on request

ISBN 978-1-84507-473-9

Illustrated with watercolour

Set in Aroma LT

Printed in Shenzhen, Guangdong, China
by C&C Offset Printing in December 2009

1 3 5 7 9 8 6 4 2

Lulu
and the
Birthday Party

Belinda Hollyer

Illustrated by Emma Damon

FRANCES LINCOLN
CHILDREN'S BOOKS

Lulu's brother Billy was having a birthday.

"When's my birthday?" asked Lulu.

"Yours is soon," said her mother.

"But not as soon as Billy's."

But Lulu wasn't listening.
She was planning her birthday party.

The next day, Lulu looked through all the letters.

She thought some of her cards might come early.
There was nothing for her.
Just some cards for Billy.

"Why has Billy got cards and not me?" asked Lulu.

"It's my birthday soon."

Her mother patted her on the shoulder. "Not yet, Lulu,"
she said. "Billy has cards before you, because his birthday
is before yours."

Lulu took no notice. She wanted her birthday to come first.

On Sunday, Lulu heard her mother
talking about a party on the telephone.

"What party?" asked Lulu suspiciously. "Is it mine?"

"It's Billy's birthday party today," said her mother.

"Remember?"

But Lulu didn't want
to hear that.
She wouldn't help,
not even with the balloons.

All Billy's friends came to the party.
They brought cards and presents
with them.

Billy's best friend Daniel gave him a wonderful new ball.

Lulu watched secretly from the hall.

And when no one was looking, she hid the ball.

Billy and his friends played all Lulu's
favourite games, but she didn't join in.
She played with her yo-yo instead.

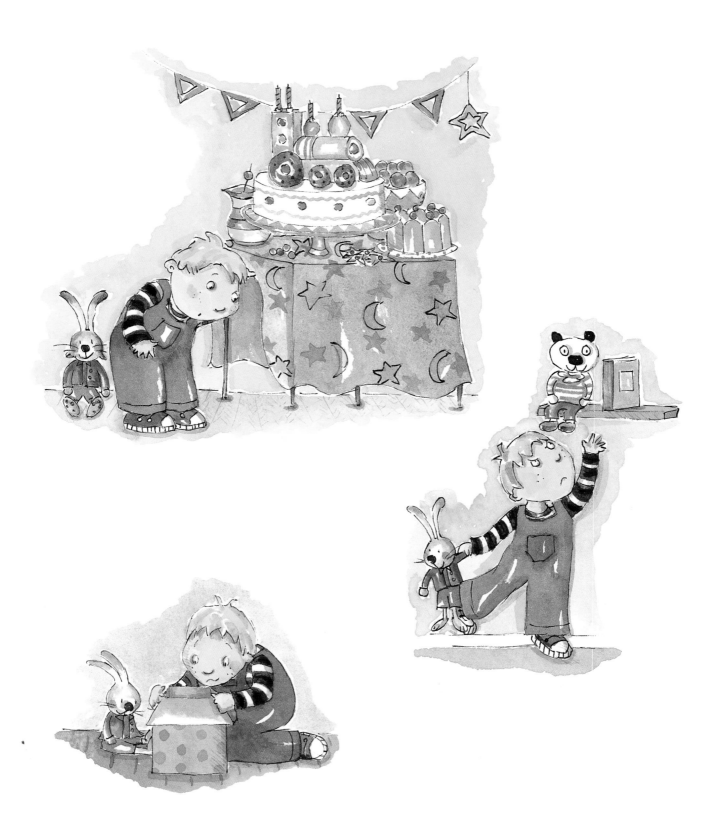

When Billy wanted to take his new ball to the park,
he couldn't find it anywhere.

He burst into tears, and everyone tried to comfort him.
Everyone except Lulu, that is.

So Billy took his kite to the park instead.
Mum and his friends went with him.

Lulu stayed home with Dad.

But when Lulu looked
around for her yo-yo,
it had disappeared.

"I can't find it anywhere!"
she said. "It's vanished!"

Dad tried to comfort her.
"Poor Lulu," he said. "That's too bad –
just like Billy's ball."

Suddenly, Lulu felt terrible.
Now she knew how Billy felt.

So she got the ball,
and took it to the park.

"I wondered where that went,"
said her mother, and gave her a hug.

Everyone played catch.
Lulu made some good shots, but Billy won.

"Well done, Billy," said Lulu.
"And happy birthday."

"But it's my birthday next, right?" said Lulu.